I0639421

Clara Florida Guernsey

The Merman and the Figure-Head

A Christmas Story

Clara Florida Guernsey

The Merman and the Figure-Head
A Christmas Story

ISBN/EAN: 9783743384125

Manufactured in Europe, USA, Canada, Australia, Japa

Cover: Foto ©Andreas Hilbeck / pixelio.de

Manufactured and distributed by brebook publishing software
(www.brebook.com)

Clara Florida Guernsey

The Merman and the Figure-Head

THE

MERMAN

AND

THE FIGURE-HEAD.

A CHRISTMAS STORY.

By CLARA F. GUERNSEY,

AUTHOR OF "THE SILVER CUP," "A MERE PIECE OF MISCHIEF," ETC.

WITH ILLUSTRATIONS.

PHILADELPHIA

J. B. LIPPINCOTT & CO.

1871.

Entered according to Act of Congress, in the year 1870, by

J. B. LIPPINCOTT & CO.,

In the office of the Librarian of Congress, at Washington.

CONTENTS.

1 *   5

THE MERMAN

AND

THE FIGURE-HEAD.

CHAPTER I.

THE SEA-NYMPH.

"I may be wrong, but I think it a pity
For a movable doll to be made so pretty."
Doll Poems.

 SHALL call her the Sea-nymph," said Master Isaac Torrey.

"Umph!" said his clerk, Ichabod Sterns, looking over his spectacles at his master.

"And why not The Sea-nymph, pray?" demanded Master Torrey. "Why, I say, should I not call my fine new brig The Sea-nymph if it pleases my fancy?"

"Fancy!" said Ichabod Sterns, putting his head on one side. "Fancy! Umph!"

Now this was most exasperating conduct on Ichabod's part, and as such Master Torrey felt it.

"Yes, if it pleases my fancy," he repeated, defiantly. "What right have you, Ichabod Sterns, to object to that, I should like to know? If I chose to name her after the whole choir of all the nymphs that ever swam in the sea—Panope and Melite, Arethusa, Leucothea, Thetis, Cymodoce—what have you to say against it? Isn't she to swim the seas and make her living out of the winds and waves? And what can you object to 'The Sea-nymph?' I'd like to hear. But it's your nature to object, Ichabod Sterns. I've no doubt that you came objecting into the world, and I've no doubt that when your time comes you'll object to dying. It would be just like you."

"And death will mind my objections no more than you, Master Torrey," said the old clerk, smiling rather grimly as Master Torrey ceased his pacing up and down the room and flung himself into a chair.

"But what *is* your objection to the name?" asked the merchant, calming down a little.

"Did I object?" said Ichabod Sterns.

"Didn't you? You were bristling all over with objections from the toe of your shoe to the top of your wig." Ichabod involuntarily put up his hand to his wig. "Why isn't it a good name for a ship?"

"Nay, I know naught against it, Master Torrey, only it is a heathenish kind of name for a ship that is to sail out of our decent Christian town of Salem."

"Heathenish! Let me tell you, Master Ichabod, that this world owes a vast deal to the heathen—more than she does to some Christians I could name."

Now this awful speech was enough to make the very pig tails of many of Master Torrey's acquaintance stand on end with horror and surprise. But Ichabod was used to his master's ways, so he did not jump out of his chair, but only looked to the door to be sure that no one had overheard the terrible statement, for had such been the case there is no telling what might have come to pass.

"How do you make that out, Master Torrey?" he said, composedly.

"Did you ever happen to hear of Socrates or Cicero?"

"Yes, I've heard of 'em," said Ichabod.

"And did you ever hear of the Duke of Alva, or Cardinal Pole, or Bloody Queen Mary, or Catenat?"

"Yes, I've heard of 'em," returned Ichabod again, a little fiercely.

"And which was the better man, the Athenian or the Christians who burnt their fellows at the stake?" said Master Torrey, triumphantly, as one who had made a point.

"Umph!" said Ichabod; "I'm not a scholar like you, Master Torrey, but I'd like you to tell me whether they were Christians by name that poisoned Socrates and murdered Cicero?"

"Well, no," said the merchant.

"Umph!" said Ichabod Sterns again, leaning back on his chair and rubbing his hands slowly one over the other.

"Well, what of that?" said Master Torrey, a little taken aback.

"Oh, nothing, sir," said Ichabod; "we have wandered a long way from the name of the new brig."

"She shall be The Sea-nymph," said Master Torrey with decision.• "What could be better?"

"I thought, Master Torrey, you might have liked to call her the Anna Jane," said Ichabod, with a little cracked laugh like an amused crow.

Master Torrey colored high, but not with displeasure.

"I wouldn't venture, Ichabod, I wouldn't dare. She's too shy, too modest, to be pleased with such an open compliment."

"Umph!" said the clerk again. It seemed to be a way he had. "But you are determined to call her The Sea-nymph, Master Torrey?"

"Ah, am I!" replied Torrey, who seemed by no means disposed to pursue the subject of the "inexpressive she," whoever it might be. "And she shall have the handsomest figure-head that Job Chippit can carve; and it sha'n't be a mere head and shoulders either, it shall be a full-length figure."

"It will cost a good penny, master. Job's prices are high."

"There's another objection! Who cares what it costs? Am I a destitute person? Am I an absolute pauper? Am I like to apply to the selectmen to be supported by the town?"

"Not yet, master," said Ichabod, gathering his papers together. "But if we go to following our *fancies*"—scornful emphasis—"there is no telling where we may end;" and without giving his master time to reply, Ichabod sped out of the counting-room.

Now I am not going to tell you a long story about Master Torrey, though I might do so if I had not a tale to tell you about something else—namely, this sea-nymph and the merman who figure at the head of this story. I was once told by a schoolmaster that in writing there was "nothing so important as a strict adherence to facts;" "fax" he called them. I treasured up this valuable precept in the inmost recesses of my mind, and I mean to adhere to facts if I possibly can. But I can't adhere to facts till I get them, and to do that I don't see but I shall have to tell you a little about Master Isaac Torrey, merchant of Salem, who was the means of putting this wonderful figure-head in the merman's way. He was a merchant of Salem when Salem was a centre of trade, and sent many a brave ship to the Indies and the Mediterranean. He was thirty-four years old, and looked ten years younger. He was a man inclined to extravagance and luxury. He wore the handsomest waistcoats and the finest lace of any one in town. He had been educated in the gravest, strictest fashion of those grave days. His parents would have been horrified if they had found him reading a novel or a play, but they urged him on to study Virgil and Homer.

Now if you will promise, my young readers, never to tell your respected instructors, I will let you into a secret. The truth is that the poems of Virgil and Homer are all full of stories as interesting and charming as any boy or girl could desire. But this is a circumstance which most school-teachers make it their first object in life to conceal, and they generally succeed so well that their pupils for the most part go through their whole course of education and never discover that their

Virgils and Homers are anything but stupid school-books—a sort of intellectual catacombs enshrining the dryest bones of grammar and parsing.

Now and then, however, a boy or girl finds out that there is food for the imagination in classic poetry. Such had been the case with Isaac Torrey, and the verses that he read with his tutor took such a hold upon him that he became what some of his friends called " half a heathen." Not but that an acquaintance with the classics was thought becoming, nay, essential, to the character of a gentleman. In the speeches and writings of those days a due seasoning of allusions to the old gods and a sprinkling of Latin quotations was considered the proper thing. But this learning was rather looked upon as solid and ponderous furniture for the mind—an instrument of mental discipline. Fancy, imagination, amusement, were ideas much too light and frivolous to be connected with anything so grave, solid and respectable as the intellectual drill for which alone Latin and Greek were intended. So when Isaac Torrey talked about the old gods as if they had been real existences, and spoke of Achilles, Hector and Andromache as though they had been live creatures, he rather startled the excellent young divinity student who was his tutor.

Once upon a time his father detecting a smell of burning followed it up to Isaac's room, where he found his son in the midst of a cloud of blue smoke. He asked the cause, and was told that in order to procure fair weather for the next day's fishing excursion he (Isaac) had been sacrificing a paper bull to Jupiter.

Mr. Torrey senior was inexpressibly shocked at the thought that his son should have been guilty of such a heathenish performance. He gave the boy a lecture of an hour long, ending with a whipping. He called in the minister to talk to him. That gentleman, on being informed of the act of idolatry perpetrated in his parish, only took a prodigious pinch of snuff and said : "Pooh ! pooh ! child's play ! child's play ! No use to talk about it. Let the boy alone." Mr. Torrey had the highest respect for his clergyman, and the boy *was* let alone accordingly, and was deeply grateful to the Rev. Mr. Bartlett.

Isaac grew up tall and handsome, went to school

and to college, and in spite of numerous prophe-
cies that he would never be good for anything,
neither went into debt nor disgraced himself in
any way.   In due course of time he succeeded to
his father's business, and astonished every one by
making money and being successful, in spite of
his tasteful dress, his "wild ways" of talking and
a report that he actually wrote poetry.

At the present time he was devoted to Miss
Anna Jane Shuttleworth, a beautiful still image of
a girl, who was supposed to have a great fund of
good sense, propriety, prudence and piety, because she liked to sit still and sew from morning
to night, and hardly ever opened her lips.   Ichabod Sterns was the old clerk of Isaac's father.   He
and his young master exasperated each other in
many ways, but they were fond of each other for
all that.

From the counting-house on the wharf and the
talk with Ichabod Sterns, Master Torrey went to
the workshop of Job Chippit, who in those days
was famous for his skill in the carving of figure-
heads.

In these times Job would probably have been a

sculptor, have gone to Rome and been famous in marble and bronze. But the idea of such a thing had never entered his brain, and he went on from year to year making his wooden figures without any thought of a higher calling. He was a little dried, brown old man, with bright eyes slightly near-sighted. Year after year he carved Indian chiefs, eagles and wooden maidens for the Sally Anns and Susan Janes that sailed from the New England ports, portraits of public men, likenesses of William and Mary. He had once made a full-length figure of Oliver Cromwell for a certain stiff-necked old merchant of Boston who called his best ship after the great Protector—a statue which every one thought his finest work. "It was so natural," said the good folks of Salem, and really I don't know that they could have said anything better even if they had been art critics and had written for the newspapers.

True it was that all Job's works had a certain live look to them that was almost startling some-times. The Indians clenched their hatchets with a savageness quite alarming; they looked as though they might open their wooden lips and whoop.   His female figures had life and character. Each governor, senator or general had his own peculiar expression and style.

Job was an artist, and, what was more, he was a well-paid artist.   He quite appreciated his own genius, and got almost any prices he liked to ask for his signs and figure-heads.   Job was the fashion, and no ship of any pretension sailed from a harbor along the coast but carried one of his masterpieces on the bow.

As Master Torrey entered his shop he was just putting the last touches of paint on an oaken bust destined to adorn Captain Peabody's little schooner, The Flora.   "So you have nearly finished The Flora's figure-head," said Master Torrey, whose tastes led him to be a frequent visitor at Job's shop.

"And a pretty creature she is," said Job, suspending his paint-brush full of the yellow-brown pigment with which he was tinging the rippled hair of the wooden lady, which was crowned with a garland of flowers carved with no mean skill.

"And the flowers !   Don't you think they are

an improvement? What did Captain Peabody say to them?"

"He didn't jest like them at first," replied Job, continuing his work. "I didn't myself, to begin with, for you know the ship is called after his wife, and nobody ever see old Mis' Peabody going round with flowers in her hair; but the captain, sez he, 'Job, I want to have you make it somethin' like what Mis' Peabody was when she was a young woman, ef you kin,' sez he. 'She was a most uncommon pretty girl when I went a-courting in Salsbury.' Well, I was kind of struck with the idee, and the next day I went to meeting, and I sot and sot, and kind of studied the old lady's face all through meetin'-time; and when they stood up to sing, the choir sang 'Amsterdam.' You know it's a kind of livening sort of hymn. The old lady, she kind of brightened up, and it seemed as if I could see the young face sort of coming out behind the old one. Thinks I, 'Job Chippit, you've got it,' and when I come home, though it was the Sabbath day, I couldn't hardly keep my hands off the tools, and the minute the sun was down I went at it. Then when you come in the next day and told me about the Flora them old folks used to think took care of the flowers and the spring, it seemed to suit so well with my notion of the old lady when she was young I couldn't help stickin' the flowers onto her head, like a fool as I was, for they wa'n't in the bargain, and I sha'n't get no extry pay for 'em.''

"And what did Captain Peabody say?" asked Master Torrey, whose own nature found sympathy in that of the artist.

"Oh, he was as tickled as could be when I'd persuaded him about the flowers. Lucy Peabody, she's been to see it. She says she expects that's the way her mother'll look when she gets to heaven, and the flowers was like the crowns we read about in the Revelations. She's an awful nice girl, Lucy Peabody. Anna Jane Shuttleworth was with her.''

"And what did *she* say?" asked Master Torrey, eagerly.

"Oh, nothing. Anna Jane don't never have much to say for herself. I told her the wreath was your notion, and she kind of smiled, but she hadn't a word to say. But look here, Master Torrey, am I to have the making of the figure-head for your new ship, and what is it to be?"

"That's just what I have come to see you about, Job," said Master Torrey. "I am going to call her the Sea-nymph, and I want you to make the most beautiful full-length figure of a sea-nymph to stand on her bow and look across the water when the brig goes sailing away into the South Seas."

"A *sea-nimp!*" said Job; "and what sort of a critter may that be?"

"Did you never hear of them?"

"Never as I know of. There's more fish in the sea than ever come out of it. I expect these nimps of yourn are some of the kind that never come out."

"You never were more mistaken in your life, Job Chippit. They have been seen on the surface of the sea over and over again. We know almost all their names, and how could they have names if they were not real beings? Answer me that!"

"Oh!" said Job, standing back to take a general survey of his wooden Flora. "They're some of them heathen young women your head is always so full of, Master Torrey?"

"Young women! Why they were goddesses, man, or a sort of goddesses. Was there not the white-footed Thetis, mother of Achilles? and did she not come to him with all her attendant nymphs —Melite, and Doris, and Galatea, and Panope?"

"I've hearn tell of *her*," said Job, touching up the wreath on Flora's head; "it's in Lycidas:

'The air was calm, and on the level brine
Slick Panope and all her sisters played.'

"Jest so; I kinder like to read that piece. It don't seem to have so very much meanin' to't, I must say, but I sort of like the sound of it. Them nimps lived in the sea, or folks thought they did, didn't they?"

"Yes, Job, as we live on the land. I'm by no means sure that I haven't heard and seen Nereides and Oceanides myself when I've been out by moonlight on the bay or round the rocks."

"I guess they never was any round these parts; it's too cold for 'em. I knew an old sailor once that said he'd seen a mermaid, but I suppose you don't want me to stick a curly fish's tail on your figure-head?"

"No, indeed. Make her full length, like the most beautiful woman you know."

"Hev' you any idee how them young women used to dress, Master Torrey?" asked the wood-carver. "I'd like to go as near the nature of the critter as I could. I must say the notion takes my fancy. It'll make kind of a variety, and it's a pretty sort of an idee to name a ship after a thing that has its life out the sea."

"I thought you'd think so," said Master Torrey, gratified. "Ichabod Sterns said it was a heathenish name for a ship that was to sail out of Salem."

"Well, you know Ichabod. He hain't got much notion of anything of that sort. But now what's your notion of these 'ere water women? Kinder cold-blooded critters they must have been, I'm thinking." There was something in this last remark which seemed to grate on Master Torrey's feelings, whatever they were.

"Why so?" he said, a little shortly.

"Oh, because it's the natur' of all the things in

the sea.   It must have been but a damp, uncomfort-
able way to live for warm-blooded folks; but tell
me what they were like, or do you happen to have
a picture of one?"

"I'm sorry to say I have not."

"Did they think they was like folks, or did
they live for ever?"

"Some said they were immortal, others that
they were only very long-lived.   Plutarch says
they lived more than nine thousand years."

"Creation!   What awful old maids they must
have been!   That's more than old Mrs. Skinner,
who was eighty-six when she married John Dick-
enson, 'cause she said she wasn't going to have
'Miss' on her tombstone if she could help it."

"But then they always remained young and
lovely, never grew old or changed.   They used to
say that whoever looked on an unveiled nymph
went mad."

"Waal, I'd risk that if I could see one.   But
they was kind of onlucky sort of critters, then,
after all?" asked Job, who seemed to be inwardly
dwelling on some thought which he was keeping
out of the talk.

"Yes, to those who approached them rashly, but they were kind to those who worshiped them with reverence and offered them the gifts they loved."

"Waal, they wa'n't very peculiar in that. The most of women is capable of being coaxed if you only go to work the right way. I don't know how it might have been with gals in the sea, but it ain't best to be too dreadful diffident with the land kind always," returned Job, with a sly smile. "But about this figure of ourn. I suppose it ought to have some kind of a light gown on, and hadn't they—them nimps?—got no emblem, nor nothing of that sort, like Neptune's trident? I'm going to make a Neptune for a ship Peleg Brag's got. Her name was The Ann Eliza. But the young woman she was named for, she up and married Jonathan Whitbeck, so Peleg, he's gont to call his ship The Neptune now. It's the only way he can think of to take it out on Ann Eliza, and I don't expect that'll kill her; but didn't these *nimps* have nothing about them to show what they were?"

"Sometimes seaweeds, or coral and shells. Sometimes they held a silver vase."

3

" Waal, I reckon I'll take the vase, if it's agreeable to you, and make her holding it out, and put some seaweed and shells and sich onto her head, and let her hair fly loose, as if the wind blew it back. She won't want no shoes nor sandals, nor nothing of that sort. What would be the use to a critter that passes its life swimming round the sea ?''

" I see you understand. You'll make her a beauty, Job ?''

"I'll do my best. You'll want her to be a light-complected young woman, I guess.''

" They say the Nereides had green hair, but Virgil says Arethusa's was golden, so we may make our nymph's that color,'' said Master Torrey, turning away to the window.

" Jes' so ; I'll go right to work. I must get Lucy Peabody to put on a white gown and come and let me look at her a little. She'll do it. She's a real accommodating girl, is Lucy.''

" But Lucy is not fair.''

" No more she ain't. Not white as milk, like Anna Jane Shuttleworth, but she's a nice, pretty girl, and will be willing to oblige me. I'd never dare ask such a thing of old Colonel Shuttleworth's daughter."

Master Torrey smiled to himself as he thought of the silent, stately Anna standing as a model in the rude shop.

"But I'll give the figure a look like Anna Jane, if I can," pursued Job. "'To my mind, she's a great deal more like some such thing than she is like a real flesh-and-blood woman."

To this Master Torrey made no answer, but smiled at the old man's folly, and passed into the street without even asking what would be the price of the wooden sea-nymph.

CHAPTER II.

THE SEA KINGDOM.

TAKE it for granted that all my readers have heard of mermen and mermaids. But in case any one's education should have been neglected, I will just say that they are like human beings, only that instead of legs they have tails like dolphins, a fashion much more useful in their element, and regarded by them as much more ornamental, than the style in which people are finished on land.

The merladies are very beautiful. They have long, golden hair, and have often been seen sitting on the rocks by the seaside, combing their locks with their golden combs and holding a looking-glass. They are also said to sing in the most charming manner. I knew a Manx woman once whose mother had seen a mermaid making her toilette. She described the sea lady as wonderfully beautiful, and "singing in a way that would ravish your heart."

"But as soon as she saw that she was watched," said Katy, "she gave a scream like a sea eagle and dived into the water. No one ever saw her again, but I've heard the singing more than once when I was young."

Concerning the kingdoms of the sea and their inhabitants Hans Anderson has written a pretty story, which I hope you have all read. The fullest account, however, that I know of the mer countries is in the Arabian Nights, Lane's translation, where you will find the story of "Abdalla of the Land and Abdalla of the Sea." It is a pity that the date and place of this interesting narration is left so uncertain, for to some minds it throws an air of improbability over the whole story; however, it is certainly the most authentic account of the world under the waters. So far as I know, "Abdalla of the Land" is the only person who has ever associated familiarly with mermen.

There was, to be sure, Gulnare of the Sea, who married the King of Khorassan and introduced

3 *

her family to that monarch. But she was not a proper merwoman, being destitute of their peculiar appendage, and being, moreover, related to the Genii and Afrites of those parts.

But in the chronicle of Abdalla you will find much that is curious and interesting. There you may read concerning the "dendan," that tremendous fish which is able to swallow an elephant at a mouthful; and, by the way, if you wish to descend into the sea undrowned, you have only to anoint yourself with the fat of the dendan. But the difficulty seems to be in catching this monster, who eats mermen whenever he can find them. You, however, are in no danger even if you happen to fall in his way, for he dies "whenever he hears the voice of a son of Adam." So if you should fall in with a dendan, you have only to scream at the top of your voice and be quite safe. But concerning these wonders and many more I have no time to write, seeing that if you can get the book you can read it for yourself.

Now there are just as many mermen and mermaids along the American coasts as there are anywhere else, though they very seldom show themselves. I heard, indeed, of a sailor who had seen one in Passamaquoddy Bay, but I did not have the pleasure of conversing with this mariner myself, so I am unable to state as an absolute fact that a mermaid was seen.

If any of you are at the seaside in the summer, you can keep a sharp lookout, and there is no telling what you may see. You would find an alliance with a mer-person very advantageous if we may judge by the experience of Abdalla. Jewels in the sea are as common as pebbles with us, and in return for a little fruit a merman will give you bushels of precious stones.

You must be a little careful, however, not to offend them, for it would seem that some of them are rather touchy and apt to be intolerant of other people's opinion in matters of doctrine and practice.

Now, not far from the Massachusetts coast, out beyond the bay, is a very beautiful sea country. There are mountains as big as Mount Washington, whose tops, just covered by the sea, are bare rock, but which are clothed around their base with the most beautiful seaweed, golden green and purple

and crimson.   Through these seaweeds wander all
manner of strange creatures, such as human eyes
have never seen, for there is no truer proverb than
that "There are more fish in the sea than ever
came out of it."   There are miles and miles of
gray-green weed and emerald moss where the sea
cows and sea horses find pasture.   There, too, are
the cities and villages of the merpeople, and
many a pleasant home standing in the midst of the
beautiful sea gardens, blossoming with strange
flowers and bright with strange fruit.

The houses are grottoes and caves hollowed out
of the rock, and for the most part very hand-
somely furnished, for there is a great deal of
wealth among the sea people.   They have not
only all the mineral wealth of the sea, but they
have all the treasures that have been lost in the
deep ever since men first began to sail the waters.
Their soft carpets are made of sea-green wool that
the sea people comb and weave, for they are skill-
ful in the arts and manufactures.

They have soft, lace-like fabrics woven of seaweed, silks and satins that the water does not hurt.
There is no coral on our Northern shores, but they

import it, and pay in exchange with oysters and looking-glasses. The sea ladies dress in the most beautiful things you can imagine, that is, when they dress at all, for in warm weather they generally make their appearance in a light suit of their own hair with a zone and necklace of pearls or jewels.

This country that I am writing about has a republican form of government, and is very prosperous and comfortable. It is a long time since any foreign power has made war upon it, and it has had time to grow and develop its resources. But at the time of which I write they had just finished a seven years' war with the king of a country lying to the east who had tried to annex the sea republic to his own dominions. This monarch had counted on a very easy conquest because the republic kept a very small army, not big enough really to keep down the sharks. Moreover, there was a large "Peace Society" in the country, every member of which had maintained repeatedly, in the most public manner, that it was the duty of every member to be invaded and killed a dozen times over rather than lift up his hand in war

C

against any creature with mer blood in his veins. The king thought this talk of theirs really meant something, and I suppose they thought so themselves in peace-times, but when the annual meeting came, about a week after the declaration of war, only two members made their appearance, and they told each other that all the men of the society had enlisted and all the women were busy making their clothes and packing their knapsacks. The king was very much surprised to find that these peaceable soldiers fought harder than any one else, and when he was at last forced to conclude peace on the most humiliating terms, it was the ex-President of the non-resistance society that insisted on a surrender of his most important frontier fortress.

"I thought you believed in non-resistance," said the king, greatly disgusted.

"So I do, your majesty, for other people," said the ex-President, respectfully, and the king had to give way.

But this is not a chronicle of the politics and history of the sea country, but only of one particular merman's fortunes. Our merman was young and very handsome, and belonged to a very distinguished family in his own state. It was said that they were in some way connected with that royal race to which belonged Gulnare of the Sea—she who married the King of Khorassan. It was whispered that the family were descended from a younger son of this pair, who had married a mer lady, and displeased both her family and his to such an extent by the marriage that they had left the Eastern seas and emigrated to the English waters, and from there into the new sea lands of the West.

All these things, if they were true, must have happened centuries before my merman was born. The legend was well known, and if it was founded on fact, the family had human blood in their veins and a cross of sea genii, for Gulnare was, as you will remember, not quite a flesh-and-blood woman. However, the humanity in them was at least royal humanity, and the King of Khorassan, as the story goes, was a very fine gentleman.

All the people of that country were fair-haired, big-boned people, with blue eyes, but the race I am writing about were black haired and dark eyed,

with slender hands.   They were rather delicate
and slight in their appearance, and they had a pe-
culiarly graceful way of carrying their tails, a
manner quite indescribable in its elegance, but a
family mark.   They were rather more intellectual
than their countrymen, and were fond of literary
pursuits and the study of magic, which in the sea
land is considered as a very essential part of a
gentleman's education.   It is taught only in the
higher schools and colleges.

Our merman's old grandfather (his father was
dead) was Professor of Magic in the State Univer-
sity, and so expert in his own science that he could
turn himself into an oyster so perfect that you
could not tell him from the genuine article.   It
was said that once while in that condition he had
been nearly swallowed by a member of the Fresh-
man class.   For this offence the young merman
was called up before the Faculty.   He apologized
very humbly, and said his only motive had been
to see if he couldn't for once get the professor to
agree with him.   He professed himself very peni-
tent, and was let off with a reprimand, but he said
afterward that his great mistake had been in wait-

ing for the pepper and vinegar. After this accident the professor could never be induced to repeat the performance except in a small circle of his intimate friends.

Now, there was one curious thing about this family, and one which makes me think there was some truth in the legend of their descent from Gulnare and the King of Khorassan.

All the other merpeople have the greatest objection to human beings, and shun all inhabited coasts, seaport towns and ships. But every once in a while a member of this race would show the oddest fancy for the shore and a kind of longing after human society—a longing which of course they never could gratify, for they could not live out of the water, and if they had been able to desert the sea, the forked ends of their long tails would have been of no use on land.

A few years before the family left the English coast, a younger son had actually married a human girl who went back to her friends and deserted him on the shamefully false pretence that she wanted to go to church. The poor merman went out of his wits and died, and was ever afterward

4

held up as an example to any of the younger ones who showed any signs of similar weakness. To care anything for human creatures is counted disgraceful in mer society, and the older members of the family for the most part felt it their duty to express the greatest possible animosity to the whole human race. The old professor of magic had once said that he would swim a hundred miles to see a shipwreck if he were only sure the people would all be drowned, but he was strongly suspected of having saved a drunken sailor who fell overboard from a Cape Cod schooner. The professor himself used to deny this story with great indignation, and say it was of a piece with the slanderous invention about his family's connection with Gulnare of the sea and her misalliance.

His grandson, however, if the story was hinted at in his presence, would look grave and say that he had never supposed the story was true, but if it were, his grandfather had only obeyed the dictates of mermanity. This was a shocking speech in the ears of the merpeople. Our young merman, however, had distinguished himself in the war, and no one cared to quarrel with him. So they contented themselves with calling him "queer," and saying that "oddity ran in the family."

It was the summer vacation in the sea land. All the commencements in the mer colleges were just over. All the presidents of those institutions had made their speeches in languages dead and alive, and told all their classes what an enormous responsibility rested upon them, how they were bound to "go forward," and "to conquer," and to "build themselves up," and to "develop themselves," and be "leaders of their kind," and, in short, do something in proportion to the expense bestowed on their education. This is a way they have in sea land. But naturally in the sea they take things cooler than we can on land, and you wouldn't believe how very little difference the advent of all these expensively got up young mermen made in the water world if you had not been there to see. Now the old mer professor hadn't had a very comfortable time. His class that year was rather a stupid one, and with all the pains he could take and all the "coaches" they could use they hadn't passed a very good examination in magic. One young gentleman upon whom he had thought he could certainly depend being told to make himself invisible, which is a very difficult problem, had made a mistake, used the wrong formula, and by accident transformed the whole Board of Examiners, who were not expecting any such thing, into cuttle-fishes. There was dreadful confusion for a few minutes, for the student couldn't remember how to turn them back again, and as the spell could not be undone by any one else, the members of the board got all tangled up together, while the professor, in an awful temper, was trying to teach the young man the right formula.

But they were all undone at last, only there was one immensely wealthy old merman who was never quite sure in his mind that he had got back his own proper curly fish's tail, and not that of some other gentleman, so that all the rest of his life he was in a puzzle as to at least half his personal identity. This incident so vexed him that he did not give anything to the college funds, as he had fully intended. This circumstance and a few other ac-

" And by accident transformed the whole board of examiners into cuttle-fishes." Page 40.

cidents had so annoyed the professor that instead of going to the North Seas with his grandson he shut himself up in the house and began to write a book. The book was in opposition to a theory put forth by a learned merman in the Baltic Sea that human beings were undeveloped mermen. The professor, however, declared that they were no such thing, but simply undeveloped walruses. He began his first chapter by saying that, while he had the highest respect for the Baltic merman's acquirements, intellect, penetration and general infallibility, he nevertheless felt himself obliged to declare that none but an idiot or a madman could come to the conclusion of the learned man aforesaid. He (the professor) wished to lay down his platform in the beginning, and state that he differed from the opinions of the learned author on this and all other conceivable points.

"You'd a good deal better go along with me, grandfather," said the young merman, swimming into the room where the professor was sitting with his big books all about him. "Think how nice and cool it will be among the icebergs this hot weather. Hadn't you better come?"

4 *

"I won't," said the old professor, snapping and switching his tail angrily round in the water, for the houses there are full of water, as ours are of air.

"I didn't say you would, sir," said the young merman ; "I said you'd better."

" Did you ever know me say I would do a thing when I did?" returned the professor, angrily. "I mean, did you ever know me say I did do a thing when I would? Pooh! Pshaw! That isn't what I mean."

"Yes, sir!" said his grandson, respectfully.

"What do you mean by that?" said the professor, sharply. "There's that catfish mewing at the door. Get up and let her in, do, and make yourself useful for once in your life."

The young merman got up and opened the door for the catfish, which came swimming in, followed by two little kitten fish. These, frisking playfully around the room, soon overset the professor's inkstand.

"There!" said the professor to his grandson. "That's all your fault! What did you let them in for? Open the windows and let in some fresh

water, do. Scat! scat! you little torments! I
don't believe the cook has given them their din-
ner; she never does unless I see to it myself; your
sisters forget them. No, I'm not going to the
North Seas; I can't spare the time."

"Don't you think you can, sir?" said the young
merman. "What odds does it make about those
forked creatures on land?"

"Do you know this fellow has the impudence
to pretend that they are undeveloped mermen,
that they'll be just like ourselves after a series of
ages when their two legs grow into one, and that
our ancestors were actually of the same type as
those low creatures that go about in ships? But
perhaps you agree with him, sir?" said the old
professor, with a look that seemed to say that if
he did he might expect to be annihilated on the
spot.

"Not I, sir. For aught I know we mermen
may be undeveloped human beings. I've sometimes thought so, I have such a sort of longing
for the land."

"How dare you—?" began the old gentleman in
great indignation.

"Come, come, grandfather," said the young merman, smiling. "You are not angry with me I know; I presume you've felt just so yourself."

The professor was silent, and swam thoughtfully two or three times up and down the room. The two little kitten fish went and sat on his head.

"I won't say but I have," he remarked at length, "but it's best not to mention it. Where do you mean to go for your vacation?"

"I thought I should go North along the coast," said the young merman. "I can't help having a curiosity about the land, and if I am in a way to observe any human creatures, I may pick up some facts to support your theory that they are undeveloped walruses."

"Any one can see that who has ever seen them floundering about in the water," said the old professor, scornfully.

"But the men drown and the walruses don't."

"That's because the men have not yet acquired the habit of not being drowned," said the professor. "When are you going?"

"To-morrow, I thought."

"Very well," said the professor. "Swim away with you now, and tell the cook to feed these kittens; there they are nibbling the hair off my head."

The next day the young merman set off on his travels. He bade good-bye to no one but his grandfather and his two sisters. His best friend was away as bearer of despatches to the secretary of state.

"I wish he wouldn't go near the coast," said the older sister, wistfully.

"So do I," said the younger; "I'm afraid for him. But, sister, now honestly, don't you wish you could see a human creature near enough to speak to?"

"No, not I," said the elder, who had less of the family traits than any of her relations; "I wish you wouldn't say such silly things."

Just as the young merman was going out of the front door, he met a huge lobster coming into it, and without ringing. The young merman felt that this was a liberty in the lobster, and was sure that his grandfather would not be pleased.

"Hadn't you better go round to the back door?"
he said, quietly.

Now the lobster was no less than the old Witch
of the Sea in disguise.

"Round to the back door indeed!" shrieked
the lobster. "Do you know who I am, young
man?"

"I beg your pardon," said the young merman;
"I had no idea you were any one in particular.
The servant will admit you if you wish to see the
professor."

"I do," said the lobster, in a huff, "but I
won't;" and she turned round and swam away.

The professor saw her out of the window. He
knew who it was well enough, but he did not like
the Witch of the Sea. He thought females had no
business to study magic, and he said she practiced
her art in a most irregular manner. Moreover,
she could do two or three things which he couldn't,
so he naturally held her in contempt.

"Ahrr! you old fool!" cried the lobster,
shaking her claw at him.

But the professor pretended to take no notice.
"Those low-bred people always call names," he

said to himself. "What an old humbug she is, and what idiots people are to go to her for advice!"

The merman went swimming on his way, but as he swam he passed a garden. It was rather a large garden, shut in by a hedge of sea flag and tangle, with pink and white shells glittering here and there among the leaves. Behind the garden was a very lofty and spacious grotto, where lived a family with whom the professor's household was very intimate. The merman paused a minute, for some one in the garden was singing. The singer had a voice that would have made people on land go wild to hear her. If you can imagine a wood-thrush multiplied by fifty and singing articulate music, you can have some idea of the mermaid's voice. But in the sea every one can sing, and they don't care much more for it than we do here for public speaking. She was singing a silly little song, but it was joined to a sweet air, and the words were of no great consequence:

" My goodman marchèd down the street,
 ' Good-bye, my dear, good-bye,' said he;
 ' Good-bye, my dear;' it might be ne'er
 Would he come back again to me.

" ' Good-bye, my love,' I said aloud;
    I kept my smile, I did not cry;
' Good-bye, my own,' and he was gone,
    And who was left so lone as I !

" It was so long, so very long,
    I kept myself so calm and still;
The days went on, the time was gone,
    I lost my hope and I fell ill.

" I could not rest, I could not sleep,
    I hid myself from every eye;
And wearing care to dumb despair
    Was changed, and yet I did not cry.

" My goodman came up the street,
    And from the street he called to me :
' Look out, my dear, for I am here,
    And safe returned to comfort thee.'

" My tears fell down like summer rain,
    I could not rise to ope the door,
Though once again, so firm and plain,
    I heard his step upon the floor.

" I was so glad, so very glad,
    I had to cry and so did he;
But wars are o'er, and now no more
    My goodman goes away from me."

"Is that you?" called the merman when the song was done.

Just over the hedge was a little arbor covered with trailing sea-plants. As the merman spoke, two little white hands parted the broad crimson leaves of a dulse that hung over the door, then there swam out one of the loveliest mermaids in the whole sea. Her yellow hair shone like gold, and was full two yards long as it trailed on the water, for mermaids never wear their hair any other way. Her complexion was like the inside of a pink-and-white shell, and her eyes were like two clear, still pools of water, they were so pure and deep. As for the mer part of her, the dolphin's tail, I declare it was only an additional beauty, she managed it so gracefully. I can't begin to tell you how beautiful she was. She was a very intimate friend of the merman's sister, and he had known her all his life—ever since they used to chase the fishes round the garden and in and out of the rocks, and make baby-houses together.

"Where are you going?" said the mermaid to the merman.

"Only North a little for my vacation trip."

"Without saying good-bye?" said the mermaid, smiling as though she did not care a bit.

"I didn't know you'd come home till I heard you singing. I sha'n't be gone long; what shall I bring you?"

"A tame seal to play with, if you can remember it."

"Tie a string round my finger," said the merman.

"You can wear this," she said, holding up a seal ring of red carnelian. "I found it in the garden; I suppose it belonged to some human being."

It was a large seal ring, having two interlaced triangles cut in the stone.

"That's a spell," said the merman; "it will keep away evil spirits."

"Then wear it," said the mermaid, holding it out to him, and he slipped it on his finger.

"Good-bye," she said; "you won't forget the tame seal?"

"Certainly not; I'll be home in time to dance at your birth-day party."

The mermaid swam away to the house, turning

at the door to wave her hand to her old playmate. but he did not see her. His two sisters had watched their interview from an upper window of their own house.

"He has no more eyes in his head than an oyster," said the elder, in quite a pet.

"It would be so nice," said the younger, with a sigh. "It would be just the thing for him."

"Of course, and that's the reason why he never thinks of it," said the elder, who had more experience.

CHAPTER III.

THE FIGURE-HEAD.

N the mean time, a most beautiful thing had grown out of the oak block in Job Chippit's shop.

Day by day Job worked at the figure-head of the Sea-nymph, Master Torrey's beautiful new brig that was lying on the stocks all but ready for the launch. Job spared no pains on his work, and his wonderful success really astonished himself.

Every one wanted to see the new figure-head, but Job kept it locked up in an inner room, and would admit no one but Master Torrey and Lucy Peabody. Lucy had been willing to put on a white dress and stand for a model, but the figure did not look at all like Lucy. It was taller, more slender, and the features were nothing like hers.

Once or twice Lucy had persuaded Anna Jane
Shuttleworth with her into Job's shop. The old
man had studied her face, and worked every moment of the young lady's stay. He stared at
Anna in meeting-time in a way that almost disturbed that young woman's composure, but she
looked straight before her and took no notice. It
was impossible to tell how she felt. Anna was
always "very reserved," people said. They had
an idea that treasures of wisdom, good sense and
virtue were at once indicated and concealed by
that statue-like air and silence.

Master Torrey was delighted with the nymph,
which was, indeed, most beautiful. She stood on
a point of rock, leaning lightly forward. Her
rounded arms upheld a silvered vase of antique
fashion; her head was thrown back; her hair,
crowned with seaweed and coral, streamed over
her shoulders as though blown by the same breeze
that wafted back the thin robe from her dainty
feet and ankles; the face was of the regular classic
type, yet not quite human in its cold purity; the
eyes looked out over the sea toward the far hori-
zon. It was really quite extraordinary how the

5 *

old Yankee wood-carver could have accomplished such a work of art. It looked, also, as if it might, if it chose, open its lips and speak, but you were quite certain it never would choose, it was so life-like and yet so still.

Job had sent to Boston and procured finer colors than he had ever used before, and laid them on with a cunning hand. He had painted the sea lady's robe a pale sea-green; over it fell her hair—not yellow with golden lights, but soft flaxen; the eyes were blue, and the faintest sea-shell pink tinged the lips and cheeks. It was altogether the most beautiful figure-head that any one had ever seen.

"There! I reckon she's about done," said Job as he laid down his last brush and stood contemplating his work. There was an odd look on the old man's face, half satisfaction, half dislike.

"She's a pretty cretur, ain't she?" he said to Lucy Peabody.

"Beautiful," said Lucy, but speaking with a slight effort.

"Don't you like her?" said Job in a doubtful tone.

"'Don't you like her?' said Job, in a doubtful tone."

"She's very beautiful, Uncle Job, but—but"—
and Lucy hesitated—"I shouldn't want any one I
cared for to love a woman like that."

"Waal, I can't say's I would myself," said Job.
"But this ain't a woman, you see; it's one of
them nimps. They wa'n't like real human girls,
you know."

"But she is not kind," said Lucy, with a little
shiver. "She would see men drowning before her
eyes, and would not put out her hand to help them.
I think she took those pearl bracelets and her necklace from some poor dead girl she found floating
in the sea. She wouldn't mind; she would only
care to dress herself with them."

"I won't say but that's my notion of her too,"
said Job. "Do you know, Lucy," he continued,
in a lower voice, "I can't help feeling as if there
was something more than common in this bit of
wood all the while I've been doing it? It seemed
as if 'twa'n't me that was making of it up, but I
was jest like some kind of a machine going along
on some one else's notion. Sometimes I am half
skeered at the critter myself."

"You meant to make her like Anna Jane

Shuttleworth, didn't you?" asked Lucy, suddenly.

"Waal, yis, I did kind o' mean to give her a look of Anna Jane, 'cause Torrey, he's so set on her, but I've got it more like her than I meant. Somehow, it seems as if it was more like her than she is herself."

Lucy gave one more long look at the figure. "I must go," she said, with a little start. "Goodbye, Uncle Job;" and she flitted away by a side door.

Just then Master Torrey came into the shop, and with him came old Colonel Shuttleworth and his daughter. Colonel Shuttleworth was a pompous, portly man, in an embroidered waistcoat, plum-colored coat and lace ruffles.

"A pretty thing! a pretty thing!" he said, condescendingly. "How many guineas has she cost Master Torrey?"

"You didn't expect I was going to make her for nothing, did you, cunnel?" said Job, who stood in no awe of the old man's wealth, clothes or title.

"No, no, of course not," said the colonel, trying to be dignified. "Um! ah! it seems to me this figure has something the look of my daughter. Anna, isn't the new figure-head like you?"

"I don't know, sir," said Anna, who had dropped into a seat and sat looking at nothing in particular.

"She's so delicate, so modest, she won't notice," thought her lover. "She is lovely, Job," he cried aloud. "You have outdone yourself. Our sea lady is no mortal, but a goddess. She has everything noble in humanity, but none of its faults or weaknesses."

"Umph!" said Job; "I don't know about that. I've heard some of them goddesses was rather queer-acted people. Anyhow, I think I'd like the women folks best, not being a heathen god myself."

"Why, Job, you don't understand your own work," said Master Torrey, half angrily. "She is too pure to be moved by our passions, too much exalted above humanity to be agitated by its troubles."

"Waal now, that ain't my notion of exaltation," said Job. "'Seems to me that's more like havin'

no feelin's at all, kind of too dull and stupid and
full of herself to keer very much about anything.
This wooden girl of ourn is uncommon handsome,
though I say it, but bless you, Master Torrey! she
hain't got no more brains in her skull than a min-
now.   She'd be a kind of dead-and-alive sort of a
critter always.   If she had a husband, she'd never
bother herself if he was in trouble.   If she had a
baby, she wouldn't care much for it, only maybe
to dress it up."

The old man seemed strangely excited in this
absurd discussion.   Master Torrey, too, seemed
much disturbed and not a little provoked.   Anna
Jane sat calm and still, and wondered whether
that light green color in the nymph's robe would
become her.   The colonel, who had not the faintest idea what the two men were talking about,
looked from one to the other uncomprehending,
and consequently slightly offended.

"Are you talking about this wooden image?"
he said, wondering.

"Yes, to be sure, cunnel," said Job, with an
odd sound between a laugh and a groan.

"Come, child, it is time to go home," said the colonel, loftily.

Anna Jane rose and took her father's arm. Master Torrey followed them out of the shop without looking back or saying good-bye to his old friend. In a strange passion, Job caught up the axe and looked at the wooden nymph as if about to dash it in pieces. "What an old fool I am!" he said. "*She* ain't only wood, and I'll get my pay for her. *Creation!* it does beat all how contrary things turn out in this world!"

The figure-head of the Sea-nymph was carried through the streets in the midst of an admiring throng and fixed securely in its place on the beautiful new brig. A few days more, and the ship was launched and slid swiftly and safely into the sea. That night it was bright moonlight. Silver-gilt ripples were rising and falling along the coast and all over the bay. Now and then a fish would jump, scattering a shower of shining drops. Everything was very still around the Sea-nymph. She lay quite by herself at some distance from any other craft. There was no one on board but an old watchman, who was fast asleep. If he had been awake, he would have seen a long, bright ripple on the water coming nearer as some sea creature cut its way swiftly toward the new craft. It was our merman, who found himself drawn toward the land by a longing curiosity too strong for him to resist.

"It is all so quiet and still," he thought. "There can be no possible danger, and I do so want to see what sort of houses these human creatures live in. There's a new ship. I'm a great mind to go and look at it. What is that standing there on the end of it?"

The merman swam on slowly, debating whether he should really go and look. Something seemed at once to warn him away and to call him forward. He could not tell what was the matter with him. Once he turned to swim away. Then he made up his mind once for all, and dashed straight on toward the ship. He said over to himself a charm his grandfather had taught him: "Aski, kataski, lix tetrax, damnamenous," words of power once written on the fish-bodied statue of the great goddess of Ephesus; but, dear me! it did him no good at all. All the while he was coming the wooden nymph stood up in her place, holding out her silver vase in both hands and looking over the sea with her painted eyes.

"What a lovely creature!" thought the merman. "She is looking at me; she holds her vase toward me."

She was doing no such thing, of course—the wooden image—but he thought she was. He did not know that she would have looked just the same way if he had been an old porpoise instead of a young merman. He swam closer and closer. The moon shone on the painted face. The ship moved gently on the water. The merman thought the lady had inclined her head. In one moment he fell desperately, helplessly, in love with the oaken nymph. It certainly must have been the doing of the old Witch of the Sea. Some influence of the kind must have been at work, or else a merman who had been to college would surely have had more sense than to become enamored of an oak block. But whether it was the witch's work, or whether it was the drop of human blood in his veins, or whether it was fate, that is just what he did—he fell in love with a wooden image. He

6

forgot his home, his old grandfather, his sisters, his best friend, who loved him like a brother and who had saved his life in the war. .As for the mermaid who had given him the ring, he never gave her a thought. He didn't care for anything in the world but that painted image smiling up there and holding its vase. He saw nothing but that, and, in fact, he didn't see that either, for he saw it as if it were alive.

"Oh I wish I knew her name or what she is!" said the merman to himself. "She can't be human. She is too beautiful." He swam round and round and read the words "The Sea-nymph" painted under the figure. He gave a jump almost out of the water. "It is a nymph," he said—"one of the Nereides or Oceanides. I thought they had left this world long ago. What can she be doing on that ship?"

He gazed at the wooden creature with all his heart in his eyes. He wished he were human that he might at least be a little like this lovely shape. He hated his own form. Was it likely the divine nymph would ever deign to notice a creature with a fish's tail? Finally he ventured to speak.

"Fairest nymph," he said.

He got no answer, but as the shadow of a cloud flitted across her face, and then the moon shone on her, he thought the nymph smiled. If there had been any possible way, he would certainly have climbed up to her, though he knew he could not live five minutes out of the water. He did not think anything about that, the poor silly merman. He was so infatuated that he would have been glad to die beside her. He stayed there the whole night talking to the wooden sea-nymph, and when the image moved with the rise and fall of the water he thought she inclined her head toward him. He said the most extravagant things to her; he told her all he had ever thought or felt, things he had never spoken to his best friend who loved him dearly; he poured out all his heart into the deaf ears of the wooden nymph. The image kept looking out over the water with its painted eyes, and the merman thought, "Now at last I have found some one who can understand me."

It was growing to gray dawn when a huge sea gull came sweeping over the water, and poised and hovered over the merman's head.

"Hallo!" said the sea-gull to the merman, "what are *you* up to, young man?"

The merman was disgusted and made no answer.

"You'd better clear out of this," said the gull. "If they catch you, they'll make a show of you and wheel you round the streets in a tub of water for sixpence a sight."

"Be so good as to reserve your anxiety for your own affairs," said the merman, haughtily. He had always been sweet-tempered, but now he felt as if he must have a quarrel with some one. He had a general impression that every living creature was his rival and enemy. He didn't just know what he wanted, but he was determined to have it.

"Highty tighty!" said the sea-gull. "Don't put yourself out. What have we here? A pretty wooden image, upon my word!" and the gull perched on the sea-nymph's head and scratched his ear with one claw. The merman went almost wild at the sight.

"You profane wretch!" he shouted; "how dare you? Oh, good heavens, that I should see her so insulted and not be able to help her. Oh, why can't I fly?"

"'Cause you hain't got no wings," said the vulgar bird, flapping his own wide white pinions. "Why shouldn't I perch here as well as on any other post? It's none of your funeral."

"Post!" said the merman, in a fury.

"Yes, post! Why? You don't mean to say you think this thing's alive?"

"Alive! She is a goddess, a nymph, an angel!"

"Well, you *are* a muff," said the gull, with immense contempt. "If I ever! Look here! if you don't want a harpoon in you, you had better quit."

"I'll wring your neck," said the merman, in a rage.

"Skee-ee-eek!" screamed the gull. "Will you have it now or wait till you get it? Take your own way, if you only know what it is;" and the gull lifted his wings and swept off over the water, laughing frantically. The wooden lady kept looking over the sea.

"What noble composure! what breeding!" thought the merman. "She scorns to notice a creature like that. How much more noble and womanly is this modest reserve and silence than the chatter and laughing of our mermaids!"

It grew lighter and lighter; sounds of life were heard from the shore; a boat put out on the bay; presently the workmen began to come on board the brig.

"Any of those human beings can speak to her," thought the merman. He was frantically jealous of an old ship carpenter with a wooden leg.

One of the workmen caught a glimpse of him. "Ho!" said he, "there's an odd fish! Who's got a harpoon?"

The merman had just sense enough left to see that if he was harpooned in the morning he couldn't court the goddess at night. He dived and swam away, for mermen, although they are warm-blooded animals, are not obliged to come up to the top of the water to breathe.

He hid all day long under the timbers of an old wharf, and when it was still at night he came out again and swam toward The Sea-nymph. Some one had covered up the figure with an old sheet to keep the dust off. The merman thought she had put on a veil.

"What charming modesty!" he said. "She don't wish to be seen by these human beings, or perhaps I offended her by my staring."

He called her every lovely name he could invent or think of. He got no answer, of course, but that was her feminine reserve, the merman thought.

"Speech is silvern, silence is golden," he said. So it went on all the time the new brig was being fitted up. The merman lived a wretched life. Two or three times he was seen and chased by the fishermen. A talk went about of the odd creature that haunted the water near the new ship. Some one was always on the lookout for him, and once he was nearly caught. They kept watch for him at night. It was only now and then that he could worship his wooden love for an hour.

All the time the old sheet was over her head, but the merman only loved her the better. He hid under the old wharf by day, for though he knew how to make himself invisible to mermen, the charm hadn't the slightest effect where Yankees were concerned. He lived on whatever he could catch, but he had very little appetite. The shallow harbor water did not agree with his constitution. He grew thin and hollow-eyed, a mere ghost of a merman, but he was constant to his wooden image.

Meantime, the ship was finished and the cargo was stowed away. One day, glancing out from his place, he saw that the nymph was unveiled and was standing in her old fashion, lovely as ever. She was looking straight at him, the merman thought. "She is anxious about my safety," he said, with delight, for he did not know that the image just looked toward the old wharf because it happened to be in the way.

"Dearest," he said, "I would follow you over the whole ocean for such a look as that!"

That night there were so many men on board the brig that the merman did not dare go near her. The next morning the ship spread her sails and went out of the harbor with a fair wind, bound for Lisbon and the Mediterranean. That same evening there was a great gathering at Colonel Shuttleworth's. Master Torrey was married to Anna Jane.

The merman followed the ship at a long distance. He dared not go too near in the daytime for fear of the harpoon that had been thrown at him once or twice. Then it came into his head that the lovely nymph was in some mysterious way held captive by these human creatures. He swore to deliver her if it cost him his life, for which he cared only as it could serve his goddess, for that she was a goddess he fully believed.

He swam in the wake of the ship, and it was very seldom that he could come up and look his idol in the face. The sailors kept a sharp look-out for him. They thought he was some sort of monster, the poor innocent merman, and had harpoons ready to throw at him whenever he showed himself. But for all this he followed The Sea-nymph across the Atlantic. He knew he was not likely to meet any of his own people, for the mer-folk avoid ships whenever they can, and do not frequent the highway between the two continents.

One day, however, he was so possessed with a desire for the sight of his love that, utterly reck-less, he swam directly before the ship and stretched out his arms to the wooden image. "I am here!

I will die for you!'' he cried, for he thought she was suffering in her captivity and wanted comfort. There was a shout from the sailors; one flung a fish spear, another fired a gun. The captain ordered out the whale-boat, and they gave chase to the merman, for such they now saw it was. It was all that he could do to get away. He was a very fast swimmer, however, and as he was not obliged to come up to breathe, they soon lost sight of him. He distanced the boat, but he found when he stopped that the bullet from the gun had grazed his shoulder, and that he had lost blood and was suffering pain. '' It is for her,'' thought the merman as he tried to stanch the blood with his pocket handkerchief.

Just then a huge sperm whale came dashing up.

''Why, what in the world are you doing here?'' said the whale, surprised. '' Have those wretches of men been chasing you?''

'' Yes,'' said the merman, his eyes flashing; ''you may well call them wretches. Do you know who it is they hold prisoner in their hateful ship? The loveliest sea-nymph in the world.''

'' How do you know?'' said the whale.

" I have seen her. I have followed her all the way from home. She stands holding out a silver vase. Every creature in the sea ought to fly to deliver her. If I was only as big and strong as you ! These men are your enemies as well as mine and hers. I know how they kill you whales whenever they can. You can sink that ship if you like and deliver the goddess."

The whale was so astonished that he had to go to the top of the water and blow. " My dear sir," said he, diving down again, " you are under some strange mistake. That is nothing but wood, that figure on the ship, as sure as my name is Moby Dick."

" You great stupid creature, where are your eyes?" said the merman in a passion, and yet he was rather struck by the whale's remarks too.

" In my head," said Moby Dick, " and I shouldn't think yours were. Why they put some such thing on all the ships—women, dolphins, what not. I've seen dozens of 'em. I know about nymphs. I used to read about 'em in the old classical dictionary in our school. Every school of whales of any pretension has one. If she was a sea goddess, do you suppose she'd stand there in all weathers? Besides, there are no nymphs."

"Then you won't sink the ship?" said the merman.

"Certainly not; she's only a merchant ship. If she was a whaler, I would with pleasure. I've done it before now, but that was in self-defence. I'm not going to drown a lot of folks because you have lost your wits. Come, come, my young friend, go home to your family. I dare say your mother don't know you're out. You are too tired to swim after that ship, and you are hurt besides. Let me take you home on my back; I'd just as soon swim your way as any other."

The merman was a little affected by the whale's tone of kindness, but he was too much possessed with his wooden love to accept the offer.

"No! no!" he cried, "I must follow her to the ends of the earth. Something tells me she will yet be mine."

"And suppose she should be?" said Moby Dick. "Why, she's only a stick cut and painted. What would the ladies of your family think if you brought home a wooden wife?"

"You are blind," said the merman, swimming away.

"You are cracked!" the whale shouted after him, but the merman was already out of hearing.

"Dear! dear!" said Moby Dick. "What a pity! If I can find any of the mermen, I'll tell them about him. He ought not to be left to himself;" and he shook his huge head solemnly and swam away in an opposite direction.

7

CHAPTER IV.

THE BEWITCHED LOVER.

FF to Lisbon went the brig Sea-nymph, and after her the poor merman. He stayed there as long as the ship stayed, hiding under boats and behind timbers, chased more than once, in danger of his life every hour, hardly able to get a glimpse of his idol. The wooden nymph stood straight up in her place, looking toward the city this time, because her head happened to be turned that way.

Once a priest going across the water in a boat happened to see him. The priest took him for a demon, was dreadfully scared, and solemnly cursed him, as is the fashion of priests when they are afraid of anything. Besides, such is the approved mode of dealing with demons in those countries. The report went abroad that there was an evil spirit in the harbor. The Spanish and Italian sailors said innumerable prayers to the saints and bought little blessed candles. The Yankees and Englishmen hunted him whenever they could, for they had a curiosity to see what a live demon was like. You may imagine what a life it was for the poor merman. He was almost worn out when The Sea-nymph weighed anchor and set sail for Sicily. He followed her, of course, for he was more possessed than ever.

And yet away down at the bottom of his heart he had misgivings. When day after day went on and the nymph stood still in the same place, he could not help thinking to himself, "What if it should be a wooden image, after all!"

But when this thought came into his head he drove it away, and called himself all the names that ever were for daring to entertain such a notion about his goddess. Was she not constant? Did she not always hold out her vase toward him? He didn't or wouldn't think, the poor silly merman, that it was because he always swam right before her and she couldn't hold it any other way.

Not far from the Straits of Gibraltar the merman met his most intimate friend, who had been looking for him a long time, and had only heard of him through Moby Dick.

"My dear fellow," said his friend, "I am so glad to see you!" and then he stopped, for he couldn't help seeing that the other was not at all glad to see him, and he felt hurt and disappointed.

"Are you?" said the merman, coldly, and gazing after the ship sailing away from him.

"Why, of course. We've all been so anxious about you. Why haven't you written? Your grandfather has tried every spell he could think of, but it all seemed of no use. The dear old gentleman is almost sick, and so miserable about you that he has had no heart to finish his work, even though the Baltic merman has come out with another pamphlet. Do come home."

Now as his friend spoke our merman felt at once how selfish and ungrateful he had been. But his passion for his wooden nymph had so altered his nature that instead of being sorry he was only angry with himself, and pretended that he was angry with his friend.

"I suppose I am old enough to be my own master," he said, haughtily.

"Why, what has come over you?" said his friend. "I'm sure it was natural I should come to look for you. If I'd been lost, wouldn't you have tried to find me?"

The merman felt more and more ashamed of himself and grew crosser and crosser. "Excuse me," he said, coldly, "but I have business that I must attend to. I don't choose to discuss the subject;" and he swam away after The Sea-nymph.

"But look here!" said his friend, coming after him. "I must tell you something. I'm going to be married to your youngest sister, and I want you to come and be best man. The girls are breaking their hearts about you."

"Oh, I dare say," said the merman with a sneer. He had always been a most affectionate brother, but now he had no room in his heart for anything but his wooden image.

"And there's a dear little girl next door that will be glad to see you. She's to be bridesmaid, of course. It's my belief she likes you. The

7 *

sweetest mermaid in the sea, she is, except your sister."

"She's well enough for a mermaid," said the merman, impatiently, for the ship was going farther and farther away.

"I think you ought to be ashamed of yourself," said his friend, growing vexed at last. "I shall really think that absurd story of Moby Dick's was true when he said you were in love with a wooden statue of a human being."

"She's not human," snapped the merman, coloring scarlet; "she's a nymph, an immortal."

"Let's have a look at her," he said.

"You are not worthy to behold her perfections," said the merman.

"Why, a catfish may look at a congressman," said his friend, quoting a sea proverb. "Is she on board that ship off there? Come on;" and away he went and our merman after him. They came up with the ship, and there, as usual, stood the wooden image staring over the water.

"She's watching for me," said the merman.

The friend said nothing. He swam round and

round, and looked up at the figure-head through his eye-glass.

" Isn't she a goddess?" asked our merman, impatiently.

"Goddess!" said the other. "My dear fellow, it's only wood as sure as you are alive."

" No merman shall insult me," said our merman, in a passion.

" Who wants to ? Do open your eyes, my dear boy, and see for yourself."

" I do ; I see how she looks at me and holds out her silver vase."

"She'll do as much for me," said his friend, swimming before the ship. Our merman was wild with rage and jealousy, for he could not help seeing that she did. He drew his sword (for he wore one), made of a sword-fish blade, and flew at his friend. "Defend yourself," he said.

" Nonsense," said the other. "A likely story, I am going to fight you about a wooden stick. As for looking at me, she'd do the same for any old turtle."

The merman couldn't but feel that this was true. But he only grew more angry. He struck his friend with all his might.   There was a dark stain on the sea.

"I'm not going to fight you," said the other, turning very pale, "for you are *her* brother, but I think you'll be very sorry for this some time;" and he turned round and swam away as well as he could.

Fortunately, after a little he met Moby Dick.

"Hallo!" said the whale in a tone of concern. "What's the matter?"

"Nothing much," said the other, for he wouldn't tell the story.

The whale suspected the truth.   He sniffed and wiped his eyes with his flipper, for he was a soft-hearted monster.

"Come with me," said he; "I'll take you to a surgeon."

He carried the wounded merman to an old sea-owl who lived in a cave under the rock of Gibraltar.   The old sea-owl was sitting in his door reading the newspaper when Moby Dick came rushing toward him, supporting in his flipper the hurt merman, who was too faint to swim.

"This young gentleman has met with an accident," said the whale to the sea-owl; "I want you to cure him." The sea-owl laid down his paper and took off his spectacles.

"What concern is it of yours?" said the sea-owl.

"That is none of your business," said Moby Dick. "Take him into the house and take care of him."

"You are weakly sentimental," said the sea-owl. "I perceive that you belong to the rose-water class. What is suffering? A mere thrilling of a certain set of nerves. It creates a sensation which we call pain. It is disagreeable. Suppose it is. Are we sent into the world only to enjoy ourselves? Enjoyment is contemptible; the desire of happiness is base, unworthy a rational being. Let us rise to more exalted feelings; let us glorify ourselves in discomfort; and if we see any one basely comfortable, let us make ourselves as disagreeable as possible, and raise him to our own platform. What possible difference does it make whether we live or die, or are cold and hungry? What odds does it make in this huge universe? Are we nothing but vultures screaming for prey?

F

Let us cultivate silence, that I may have the talk
all to myself;" and the sea-owl looked at Moby
Dick in the most impressive and superior manner.
" What difference, I repeat, does our happiness or
misery make in the huge sum of the universal—?"

"Look here!" said Moby Dick, "if you don't
quit talking and tend to this young man, I'll swallow you.   I don't know as that will make much
difference in the universe, but it'll make a sight
of difference to *you;*" and the whale opened his
tremendous jaws wide and showed all his teeth.

The sea-owl took the merman into his office on
the instant. He bound up his wound and attended
him very carefully, for he was by no means such a
fool as you would imagine from his conversation.
The merman was cured before long, and made the
sea-owl a handsome return for his services.   The
owl was just as much pleased as though the money
had been a large item in the sum of the universe.
He gave the merman a present of his own poems
neatly bound in shark skin.   He had several hundred copies in his office, for he had issued them at
his own expense.   They had been much praised,
but some way they did not sell.   The sea-owl said

it was because all the people in the sea were "Phil-
istines." No one knew just what he meant, but
when he called people by that name most all of
them experienced a sort of crushed feeling, and
pretended to admire the poems. Sometimes they
would even buy them, but not often. Moby Dick
accompanied the young merman home, and they
made up a story that his hurt had been caused by
a sword-fish, against whom he had run in the dark.
Nobody believed him, for some way every one
knew the truth, but all the members of the family's
own circle pretended to believe the tale, for they
were all very high-bred people.

It had been intended that the wedding of the
professor's granddaughter should be a very bril-
liant affair, but they felt so unhappy about the
grandson that they resolved to invite only a few
intimate friends. Moby Dick, of course, was
among the number. He was too huge to come
into the house, but he put his nose to the window
and ate ice cream with a fire shovel for a spoon.
The beautiful mermaid from next door was bridesmaid, and looked most lovely. She seemed in
better spirits than any one else, and never said a

word about her old playmate. Toward the end
of the evening she went out into the garden that
was all glittering with sea phosphorescence. She
swam up to Moby Dick and said it was warm
weather.

" So it is, my dear," said the whale, and looking with admiration at the bridesmaid, who wore
white lace and emeralds.

" You came from Gibraltar, didn't you?" said
the mermaid, playing with her looking-glass, which
the sea ladies carry as ours do their fans.

" Yes, where the bridegroom and I went to see
after that bewitched brother-in-law of his," said
the whale, for he was vexed at the merman.

" Do you think he is bewitched?" said the
bridesmaid.

The whale scratched his head, which is not vulgar in a whale.

" I never thought of it before," he said ; " but
now you speak of it I shouldn't wonder if it was
so."

The bridesmaid whispered in the whale's ear.

" I wish you'd come with me to the old Witch
of the Sea," she said.   " Won't you, please?"

"I'll go to the ends of the ocean with you, miss, if you want me to," said Moby Dick; "but what for?"

"Oh," said the bridesmaid, looking straight in the eye which happened to be that side of the whale's head, "I'm a friend of the family, you know. I'm very much attached to the girls and very fond of the professor. I should like to help them if I could, and I think the witch is a wise woman, and it wouldn't do at all for the professor to go to her in his position, but it won't make any difference to me and you. Will you come now? It isn't far."

"Of course I will," said the whale. "Just sit on my head, and I'll take you there in no time."

Just then the bride's sister came out into the garden.

"Are you going, dear?" she said to the bridesmaid.

"Yes, I think I shall. Mr. Dick will see me home," said the other mermaid.

"It's been rather forlorn," sighed the bride's sister. "To think of his loving a wooden thing!"

"I suppose he had a right to if he chose," said

8

the mermaid a little hastily. "I'm sure it's nothing to me."

The bride's sister was not angry at all. She kissed her friend good-night, and when she and Dick had gone sat down and cried a little.

"The poor dear!" she said.

Meanwhile Moby Dick and the bridesmaid were on their way to the old Witch of the Sea. She lived in a cave in a thick dark grove of seaweed. She was sitting before the door talking with a gossip of hers, one of the Salem witches, whose broomstick would carry her through the water as well as through the air. The broomstick, which was a spirited young one, was standing hitched at the door, impatiently stamping its stick part on the ground and switching the broom part about to keep off the little crabs.

"Ho! ho!" said the Salem witch. "Here's a dainty young maiden indeed! I'm a great mind to stick a few pins in her."

"You better hadn't," said Moby Dick, grimly, for he was not at all afraid of witches. "Ask the old lady any questions you like, my dear; nothing shall hurt you."

"If you would be so good," said the mermaid, taking off her jeweled necklace and zone and holding them out to the witches, "will you tell me where the professor's grandson is, and whether he cannot be induced to come home?"

"And what's your interest in *him?*" said the Witch of the Sea, taking snuff and looking at her sharply.

"I am his sister's friend," said the mermaid, steadily; "otherwise it is not a matter of consequence to me whether he spends his life in the chase of a wooden image; but I am very fond of the professor, and I think it a very sad thing that he should be left alone in his old age."

"Umph!" said the Salem witch. "Just the same, fish-tailed or two-legged, in the sea or out of it. There's a girl in our town as like her as two peas."

"Young lady," said the Witch of the Sea, "I haven't had any hand in this matter." (But of course I can't say this was true. I incline myself to think she had had her finger in the pie.) "I can't undo the spell—not now. If you want to find your friend's brother, you must go West toward the coast.''

"Take a bee line," said the Salem witch.

"I don't know what that is," said the mermaid, who didn't know what a bee was.

"As the crow flies," said the Salem witch.

"Crow?" said the mermaid, perplexed.

"As the mackerel swims," said the sea witch.

"Oh, I see," said the mermaid. "Thank you very much. Pray keep the stones. Good-night;" and she turned to Moby Dick. "You'll go with me?"

"To be sure," said the whale. "That's rather a dangerous coast for me," he thought to himself. "But never mind; if they come after me I can sink a whaler as easy as nothing. I'll go with her. She reminds me of a whaless I used to go to school with;" and Moby Dick looked at the little slim mermaid in her bridesmaid's dress, and heaved a sigh about a quarter of an acre in extent. "I'm your whale," he said, cheerfully; and away they dashed at the rate of a hundred miles an hour.

Every one in the sea knew that the professor's

grandson had fallen in love with a wooden image, and was following it about the world. The very porpoises talked about it to each other. The whole family were dreadfully mortified.

"Suppose he marries her!" said his sisters.

"We never can take her into society. A real human being would be bad enough, but a wooden one—"

"I disown him," said the old mer professor. "I desire that no one will mention him in my hearing. If he would only come home, the poor dear boy!"

There was universal sympathy with the family. The very sophomores behaved like gentlemen for as much as a week, they were so touched with the old mer professor's trouble.

8 *

CHAPTER V.

THE SEA-NYMPHS.

AFTER his friend had left him, our merman swam once more after The Seanymph. He felt wicked, ashamed, remorseful and very miserable, but for all that he followed his wooden goddess. He was so worn out with his long journeying and with trouble of mind that he could not keep up with the ship—he who had once beaten a fin-back whale in a race. He had lost sight of the brig before she went into the harbor of Syracuse, but he knew where she was going, and he followed in her track. It was a beautiful moonlight night. The water was all golden ripples. The ruins of the ancient town stood up white, still and solemn in the flood of silver light. The modern city did not look dirty as it does by sunlight, but white and cool and still. Only a bell rung at intervals from the tower of a convent.

On a fragment of a broken capital that lay in the water near the island shore of Ortyggia sat three lovely ladies. They looked young and beautiful as the day, but they were very, very old. They had known the place before the first Greek ship bore the first Greek colonists to Sicily. The broken capital was the last bit of a temple that had been reared in their honor ages ago, for these were the real sea-nymphs. They had come back from the unknown countries where they went when men forgot them, and the monks shattered their beautiful marble statues to replace them with waxen virgins dressed in tinsel. They were taking a journey just to see what sort of a place this world had grown to be. They were all three rather low-spirited—as much so as sea-nymphs can be.

"This is all so different," said Arethusa. "It was hardly sadder in the great siege; I could hardly find the place where my fountain was once."

"And nothing of Alpheus?" said Cymodoce with a little smile.

"No, thank Heaven!" said Arethusa; "the stream is there, but it has another name. I wonder what has become of the old gentleman? My dears, you can't think what a torment he was. I really don't know what I should have done but for Diana."

"Maybe you would have married him," said Panope. "He was very devoted to you."

"Not he," said Arethusa. "He was determined to have his own way, but he didn't get it."

"Sing something," said Cymodoce. "What concerts we used to have on this very shore! Oh dear!"

Arethusa began to sing. I only wish **you** had been there to hear her.

"Years ago when the world was young,
　And this weary time was yet to be,
A little bay lay the hills among
　Where the hills slope down to the sand and sea.

"The shepherd came down to the cool seashore,
　Fearless and tall and fair was he;

Careless the cornel spear he bore,
  As he paced the sand along the sea.

" Low in the sky the red moon hung,
  The wind went wandering wild and free;
To and fro the foam-bells swung
  Off from the sand into the sea.

" 'Come up, my love,' he called, ' oh come!
  Give, oh goddess, once more to me
That fairest face in the whitening foam,
  On the pebbly marge 'twixt the sand and sea.'

" The sunset faded like smouldering brand,
  And never the nymph again saw he;
The shadow sloped from the tall headland
  Off from the sand, out o'er the sea.

" His was a being that, born to-day,
  Grows old to-morrow and dies, and she
Lived on for ages as fair alway,
  To sing on the shore 'twixt the sand and the sea.

" Yet oh, my lover, by this right hand,
  It was fate, not I, that was false to thee;
For thine was the life of the solid land,
  And I was a thing of the restless sea."

As Arethusa finished her song, the merman came
swimming wearily toward the three nymphs. If

he had been a human being, he would not have seen them, but as it was they were revealed to his eyes. He knew what they were in a moment. They were dressed like his wooden nymph, and Arethusa carried a little silver vase in her hand, but they were not like the figure-head, for they had sweet, kind faces, and could laugh and cry. The merman made a most respectful bow, for he knew how to do it.

"Well," said Panope, kindly, "can we do anything for you?"

"Lovely nymphs," said the merman, "have you seen a ship pass this way with one of your fair sisters on its prow?"

"One of *our* sisters?" said Arethusa, a little haughtily. "That seems very unlikely."

"I assure you she is, my lady," said the merman, reverently but firmly. "She has her name, The Sea-nymph, written below her."

"He has lost his wits," said Panope, sighing. "What a pity! Such a handsome youth!"

"You don't mean that wooden figure-head?" cried Arethusa.

"Surely she is your sister," said the merman,

looking at Cymodoce, who was more like the wooden nymph than the other two, and whose manners were always a little stiff and prim.

" My sister !" cried Cymodoce, quite bristling. "Am I related to a log of wood?"

Here Arethusa slyly pinched Panope behind Cymodoce's back, for the truth was Cymodoce had once been a wooden ship, and had been made into a nymph to save her from a conflagration. She never would allow, however, that this was a true story.

" No, of course there is nothing wooden about you, dear," said Panope, soothingly. "Don't be vexed. Let us help the poor boy if we can."

" He's very like a Triton I used to know," said Arethusa, aside.

"I saw a ship pass," said Panope, looking down at him with her kind blue eyes. "Such a big ship! Not like the ones I used to see here years ago, and it certainly had a wooden statue on the prow, but it was only a wooden image; it was not alive."

" How strange it is," thought the merman to himself, " that these three goddesses should be jealous of my beauty—just like three mortal mermaids.''

''Jealous of that stick indeed !'' cried Cymodoce, answering his thought.

''Men !'' said Arethusa.   ''Panope, my darling, they are just the creatures they always were in the water or out of it.''

''So it seems,'' said Panope, playing in the sand with her little pink toes like a mortal girl.

''I assure you, sir,'' said Cymodoce, gravely, ''that you are under a serious mistake.   That figure is a mere painted figure-head, quite incapable of a rational thought or instructive conversation.''

''What we admire in woman is her affections, not her intellect,'' said the merman.

''Look at me !'' said Arethusa; and the tall nymph stood up before him in all her immortal beauty and shook down her golden hair till it swept her ankles.

''My dear Arethusa,'' said Cymodoce, ''let me ask you to consider if this is quite proper?''

Panope only smiled, and Arethusa took no sort of notice.

"Look at me," she said, "and compare me with that wooden thing. Don't you see the difference?"

A difference there certainly was. The merman felt a cold chill go to his heart. For one instant his eyes were opened; for one instant he knew he had been worshiping a stick. Then he would *not* see or feel the truth.

"Farewell!" he cried, desperately; "I will follow her to the ends of the earth, whether she is alive or not;" and he swam away.

"Poor fellow!" said Arethusa.

"He looks a good deal like the pious Æneas," said Cymodoce, who often mentioned that gentleman.

"I don't see it," said Panope, almost sharply. "He may be a goose, but he is not a prig. I do wish you ever could talk about any one else, Cymodoce! I am tired to death of the pious Æneas."

"So am I," said Arethusa; "he was a humbug if ever there was one."

"What an expression!" said Cymodoce.

"Never mind," said Arethusa; "suppose we do this poor merman a good turn, and get Aphrodite to make his wooden thing a live creature. Don't you think she would do as much for wood as she did for marble?"

"We could ask her," said Cymodoce. "I have some influence with her. I was so well acquainted with her son, the pious—"

"Oh bother *him!*" said Arethusa, who had been a mountain nymph originally, and was apt to be a little brusque.

"I don't believe she'd be good for much if she did come alive," said Panope, looking down. "I've heard that match of Pygmalion's didn't turn out very well. I saw the marble woman once. She was pretty enough, but *so* stiff, and she walked as though she weighed a ton, and hadn't a word to say for herself. And as for this wooden thing, the woodenness would always remain in her mind and manners. But we can try. Come, if you like;" and the three slipped into the sea and went swimming after the merman, but he never saw them. He had caught sight of his wooden goddess, and had no eyes for the real ones. He thought he had never seen his idol looking so beautiful, so lifelike. "*She* wood!" he thought as he leaned back in the water and looked up in her face. Meanwhile, some strange influence was at work upon the wooden image. A kind of thrill ran over it. It began slowly to breathe.

"Dear me!" thought the wooden creature, for it could think a little now. "I must be coming alive! How very disagreeable! I can see—even feel. I don't like it. It's too much trouble. What is that thing in the sea staring at me?" and she actually bent her head and looked down.

The merman, of course, was in ecstasies, for he thought she was coming to him.

"I certainly am growing alive," thought the wooden thing. "I won't come alive; I was made wood, and wood I'll stay; I won't go out of my sphere; I'm sure it's not proper;" and she stiffened herself as stiff as she could. "I will be wood," she thought, and wood she was, for even a goddess can't make a thing alive against its own will. "Yes, this is much the best way," was the wooden image's last thought, as the breath of life went away from her and left her more wooden than ever.

"Let it go, the stupid thing," said Arethusa in

a pet which was scarcely reasonable, as the image was wood in its nature. "Come, my dears, let us go from a world where no one cares for our gifts. Don't cry, Panope dear. There are just as many fools in the world as ever there were, for all they pretend to be so much wiser."

"It is strange too," said Cymodoce, "considering how long they have had before them the example of the pious Æneas—"

"*He* never lost sight of his interest," said Panope. "I wish we could persuade that poor merman, but I know very well that the twelve great gods couldn't do it;" and the three vanished and were seen no more.

That night there came up a terrible storm. There was wind and rain and thunder such as the merman had never heard. From far away came a thick sulphurous cloud of smoke, and in the air was a dull red glare. The land shook and trembled, for Ætna was feeding his hidden fires, filling his inmost furnaces. The gale blew fiercely from land. The Sea-nymph snapped her cable, and drove out of the harbor before the tempest.

The merman followed her. By the glare of the lightning he could see that the figure stood in its old place holding out her silver vase. "What wonderful courage!" he thought, for he did not know it was nailed there. The masts went crashing into the sea. The sailors threw overboard everything they could to lighten the ship. One of them sprang forward with an axe and began to cut away the figure-head. The merman swam, balancing himself on the crest of the waves; every one was too busy to notice him; he could not hear the blows of the axe in the noise of the wind and thunder; he did not see what the sailor was doing; he saw the image quiver under the strokes of the axe, and thought that at last she was coming down to him. "Oh come, come," he cried, swimming directly below and holding out his arms. The wooden image quivered and shook; it bent forward; the next instant the solid heavy oak fell with a plunge and struck the poor merman in its fall. He felt that he was dying, but he did not know what had hurt him. "My own love, my sea-nymph," he murmured; and he put his arms round the figure-head that was bobbing up

9 *

and down in the sea quite unconcernedly. He kissed the painted lips. Then at length he knew that his idolized nymph, for whom he had given his life, was nothing but a carved log. It was well for him that his next breath was his last.

CHAPTER VI.

LUCY PEABODY'S DREAM.

OBY DICK went on his way, "emerging strong against the tide." A Nantucket ship saw him as he blew, and her boats put out after him.

"Just get off a minute, my dear," said he to the little mermaid whom he carried. She did so, and then, instead of swimming away from the boats, he put down his enormous head and went straight at them.

"The white whale!" cried the sailors; and they did not throw the harpoon, but went meekly back to the ship. They were bold enough, but they were afraid of the white whale, for Moby Dick had sunk two or three ships in his time and entirely reversed the whalers' programme.

Moby Dick executed a huge frisk on the surface

of the sea, flapped his tail on the water with a noise like thunder, and then dived down to rejoin the mermaid.

"All right, my dear," he said, cheerfully.

"I'm so glad you are safe," said the mermaid, patting him with her little hands.

On they went through the water, and the coast was soon in sight. It was growing dusk, and the lighthouse showed its red star over the sea. The mermaid was silent, and Moby Dick did not trouble her to talk.

Suddenly a beautiful woman appeared to them on the crest of a long rolling billow. She made no effort; she did not swim, but moved through the water by her will alone. She seemed a part of the sea, like a wave come alive.

"That is not a human being, surely," said the mermaid, startled.

"It's very like that—you know—that wooden thing—that *he* ran after," said Moby Dick in a gigantic whisper, "only it's alive."

"She don't seem as though she could ever have been wood," said the mermaid. "She looks kind.

"'My dear,' she said, very gently, 'your old playmate is dead.'"

I don't feel as though she were that—that person. Please ask if she has seen our friend."

" Yes, my dear child," said Panope—for she it was—answering the mermaid's thought, " I have seen him ;" and the immortal sighed.

" His family are very anxious about him, my lady," said the whale, who was conscious of an awe he had never known before, though he felt he could trust the Sea-Nymph.

"They need be anxious no more," said Panope, gently and sadly.

" What has happened ?" asked the mermaid, turning pale, but keeping herself very quiet.

Panope went to her, and the immortal daughter of the sea put her white arms round the mermaid and held her in a close and soft embrace.

" My dear," she said, very gently, " your old playmate is dead."

" You don't say so, ma'am !" said Moby Dick, with a great sigh ; and then he swam away to a little distance and left the mermaid to the care of the Sea-Nymph, for he was a whale of very delicate feelings.

The mermaid looked into the blue eyes of the

Goddess, and felt that the countless ages of her being had but made her more wise and kind. She hid her face on the immortal maiden's bosom.

"My sweet child," said Panope, after a little while, "I cannot bring your friend to life—it is beyond my power—but if you will, I can give you an immortality like my own. I can carry you with me to a world where death or pain has never come, and keep you young and lovely for ever."

The mermaid was silent a moment. Then she looked up into Panope's face.

"You will not be angry with me?" said she.

"Angry, my poor darling!"

"Then, my friends that I have loved have all been mortal. My mother is dead, my twin brother was killed in the war, and now my old companion—and I have known him so long! I think I should rather not be so very different, but go to them when my time comes."

Panope caressed her hair with a soft hand.

"I don't know but you are right. Sometimes," said the Goddess, with a sad, tired look in her eyes, "I think I would be glad to be mortal myself, except that I am glad to be a little comfort to you.

I am sorry I came back. Either the world has
grown a sad place, or else I had forgotten what it
used to be. But I don't know; I almost broke
my heart over Prometheus when I was quite a
young thing. I could have helped him take care
of his beloved human race a great deal better than
Asia, but he never cared anything for me. It is
all over long ago. Is there nothing that I can do
for you, my dear?"

The mermaid was silent a minute. Then she
said :

"I think I should like to take him home to his
friends. I know they would wish it should be so."

"It shall be," said Panope. "Wait here, and
I will bring him to you. But, my dear child, you
are so quiet. All the mortal women I ever knew
in the old days, in the sea or out, would have torn
their hair and screamed, but you are so different."

The mermaid looked up with a little ghost of a
smile, half proud, half pitiful. "I suppose it is
because I was born in American waters," she said.

"Wait but a little," said Panope. "The whale
will take care of you. He is a good creature.
His great-grandfathers were pets of mine long ago.

I will soon come back again;" and the Nymph was gone.

Some time after the news had come to Salem of the total loss of the brig Sea-nymph, Lucy Peabody was walking alone along the sands. She felt weary, and sat down under the shadow of a rock to rest. The sun was just setting, the west was suffused with a golden glow, the water lay, hardly rippling to a low whispering wind, a sea of fire and glass. Lucy leaned her head against the rock, and sitting there, she dreamed a dream. Along the sands toward her came old Goody Cobb, whom everybody suspected of witchcraft. She appeared so suddenly that Lucy in her dream thought she had come out of the sea.

"Ho! ho!" said Goody Cobb, with a cracked laugh; "so here is Madam Peabody's lady daughter come out to cry over her disappointment all by herself? The man was a fool, sure enough, but I wouldn't mind. Just let me write your name down in a little book I keep, and you shall see our fine young madam dwine away like snow in spring-time, and then we shall see—"

"You are out of your mind, Goody," said Lucy in her dream; "but such talk as that is not safe, for there are those in town who are silly enough to believe witch stories, and you might get yourself into trouble."

"Silly, are they!" cried Goody Cobb, growing angry. "But never mind. Just let me have your name, and we shall see what we shall see. Look at the pretty necklace I will give you;" and she drew from her pocket a chain of shining green stones and held it up before the girl's eyes.

"I will have nothing to say to you or your gifts," said Lucy, steadily. "Pass on your way, Goody, and leave me alone."

"So you think yourself too good for me!" said the witch in a rage. "Let me tell you that my family is as good as yours, and better. My grandfather was a minister—ay, and a noted one—while yours was selling clams round the streets."

It was a very odd thing that while Goody Cobb had become a witch, renounced her baptism and sold herself to the enemy of mankind, she was yet very proud of the eminent divine, her grandfather.

"I'll be the death of you! I'll stick pins in

10

you, and set my imps to pinch you black and blue!" screamed Goody Cobb, with the look of a possessed woman, as she was.

Suddenly, as Lucy dreamed—so suddenly that she seemed to grow out of the air—there stood on the sand between herself and the witch a tall and beautiful woman in shining raiment of green and silver, with golden hair that fell loosely to her ankles. She gazed sternly on the witch; a divine wrath made her blue eyes awful.

"You earth-born creature!" she cried as she caught the green necklace from the old woman's trembling hand. "This girl is a child of the ocean, and is in my care;" and Lucy dreamed that she felt glad to remember how she had been born on the voyage her mother made with her father to Calcutta. "Stay where you are for ever!" continued the stranger lady, raising her white hand with a gesture of command. "You will wreck no more ships—you, nor your sister witch." And then as she stood Goody Cobb stiffened into stone and became a black rock.

"You need not be afraid of me, my dear," said the dream lady to Lucy. "I never hurt any one in my life. I am only an innocent Sea-Nymph, and I am—or I was—the helper of all the sailor-folk, and your father is a bold seaman.''

Lucy dreamed that she was very much surprised, which was curious, for in a dream the more remarkable a thing is, the less it astonishes the dreamer.

'' But I thought there never were any nymphs,'' she said, perplexed.

The sea-maiden smiled a queer little smile— half sad, half amused.

'' Do you know,'' she said, ''that since men left off believing in them and building temples, the gods all declare that there never were such things as human creatures, and that it was all a delusion of ours? Keep this;'' and she dropped the necklace into Lucy's lap. '' It belonged to one who will not care to wear it now. Farewell;'' and the goddess bent down and lightly kissed the girl's forehead, and the next instant Lucy was alone. She woke up, as she thought, and sat still for a moment.

'' What a singular dream !'' she said to herself. Then she looked round, and saw a black rock

standing beside her. "Was that rock there? I
don't remember it, but of course it must have
been." She rose to her feet. Something fell glittering on the sand. She picked it up. It was a
long, shining necklace of green stones.

"This is very strange!" said Lucy, thoughtfully.
"But I suppose I had better take them home.
They must have been washed up from the sea and
caught to my gown some way. How pretty they
are! I wonder if they belonged to some one who
is drowned?"

She put the necklace into her pocket, and turned
to go home. She had gone but a little way when
she met Job Chippit.

"Uncle Job," she said, "I have found something on the sand. Do you think any one in town
has lost it, or that it was washed up by the sea?"

Job examined closely the emerald necklace.
"This never belonged to any one in our town,
Lucy," he said; "most likely the tide washed it
up in the last storm. Yours it is by all right if no
one comes to claim it; and be keerful of it, for I
expect it's awful valuable. But what's happened
to you?"

"Why?"

"You've got an odd look about you, some way, but I never see you look so pretty. Has anything happened?"

"No," said Lucy, quietly, "only I sat down to rest and fell asleep, and had a very strange dream. Good-night, Uncle Job." From that evening Goody Cobb was never seen in Salem town.

Job Chippit continued his walk, thoughtfully whittling a little stick. Before long he overtook Master Isaac Torrey, who was walking along the shore with his head down, seeming to notice nothing but the sand at his feet. Master Torrey had quite left off his wild ways. He made no more foolish, fanciful speeches about nymphs and goddesses, and such nonsense. "Anna Jane had made a sensible man of him," said his father-in-law. "He was greatly improved," said every one, with the exception of Ichabod Sterns and Job Chippit.

Master Torrey had avoided the wood-carver since his marriage. His father-in-law thought it a good sign. "He had been quite too familiar with that person," thought the colonel. But this

10 *   H

night Master Torrey did not avoid him, though he only nodded without speaking in answer to Job's "Good-evening," and then the two walked on in silence.

"That's an odd-looking thing on the beach," said Job at last.

They went up to the dark mass Job had pointed out. There on a heap of weed, thrown up by the late storm, lay the wooden nymph, the paint almost washed away, and there, with its arms tightly clasped about her neck, lay a strange creature, half fish, half human.

"As sure as the world, it's a merman!" said Job; "and there really are such critters, after all! Poor fellow! The human part of him was pretty good-lookin' when he was alive. See what a dent he's got in his head!"

"And this is the figure-head of The Sea-nymph," said Master Torrey. "Don't you know it?"

"To be sure! Well, it does beat all! What shall we do with the merman? I'd kind of hate to make a show of him. He's a sort of man, and I 'spose he had his feelings anyhow. Look at the empty scabbard and the sword-belt; and he's got a ring on his finger."

Job bent down and tried to unfold the dead hand from its close clasp. At that moment, though it was very calm, a huge wave rose from the sea, and came thundering up the beach, covering the two men with spray. When it retreated the dead merman and the figure-head were gone, and up from the sea came a low sobbing sound.

Master Torrey and Job stood watching, surprised and startled. Another minute, and up came a second huge wave, bearing upon its crest the oaken sea-nymph. On it rolled—a mountain of water. It dashed its burden upon the jagged rocks once, twice, thrice, and strewed the shattered fragments over sea and sand. Job drew a long breath.

"Waal," said he, "there goes the best piece of wood I ever chipped. Tell ye what, philosophy won't explain everything. 'Tain't best to be too rational if you want to have any insight into things in *this* world. If that wa'n't done a-purpose, I never see a thing done so!"

They turned back and walked toward the town.

Far away in the offing a whale sent up an enormous jet, a sea-gull screamed wildly above their heads.

"Going to say anything about this?" said Job at last.

"What would be the use?" said Master Torrey, sharply. "Half of them would not believe you; and who wants to set all the fools in the place chattering?"

"Not I! I'm not over-fond of answering questions. I'd rather ask 'em," said Job. "Do you know, putting this and that together, and the story of the queer fish that hung round the ship, I've got a notion that poor fishy thing fell in love with that figger-head of ourn? You couldn't expect such a critter as he was to have more sense than a landsman, and I expect the log fell on him when the brig went to pieces and killed him."

"So much the better for him if he had given his soul to a wooden image," said Master Torrey, bitterly. "Good-night;" and he left Job and walked slowly back to his handsome new house. Job looked after him wistfully. Just then old Ichabod came up and saluted the wood-carver.

"Do you know, Ichabod," said Job, "that Master Torrey and I just found the figure-head of the poor Sea-nymph, all shattered to bits on the rocks? The waves brought her all this way to smash her at last."

"I wish they had smashed her at first," said Ichabod.

"Why?" said Job, with a curious look.

"Because," said Ichabod, "she was an un-lucky creature from the first. She was too much alive for a wooden image, and too wooden to be a live woman, much less a goddess."

Juvenile Publications

OF

J. B. LIPPINCOTT & CO.,

PHILADELPHIA.

———◆◆———

For sale by all Booksellers, or will be sent by mail, postage free, on receipt of price.

———◆◆———

ARTHUR'S ALL'S FOR THE BEST SERIES. In handsome box, containing: All's for the best; Heroes of the Household; The Seen and the Unseen. By T. S. ARTHUR. 3 vols. 16mo. Illustrated. Extra cloth. $2.25.

ARTHUR'S NEW JUVENILE LIBRARY. In box, containing: Who is Greatest? The Poor Wood-Cutter; Mr. Haven't-Got-Time; The Wounded Boy; Uncle Ben's New-Year's Gift; Pierre, the Organ-Boy; Who are Happiest? Maggie's Baby; The Peacemakers; The Lost Children; Our Harry; The Last Penny. By T. S. ARTHUR. 12 vols. With seventy-two Illustrations. Cloth, gilt back. $7.50.

BOYS' GLOBE LIBRARY. (FIRST SERIES.) In handsome box, containing: Sandford and Merton; Robinson Crusoe; The Arabian Nights' Entertainments; The Swiss Family Robinson. 4 vols. 12mo. Each with six Steel Plates printed in colors. Extra cloth. $6.00.

CASELLA ; or, The Children of the Valleys.
By MARTHA FARQUHARSON, author of "Elsie Dinsmore," etc. 16mo. Cloth. $1.50.

"A lively and interesting story, based upon the sufferings of the pious Waldenses, and is well written and life-like."—*Boston Chr. Era.*

"It is rich in all that is strong, generous, and true."—*Baltimore Episc. Methodist.*

"The story is one of the most interesting in ecclesiastical History."—*The Methodist.*

DEEP DOWN. A Tale of the Cornish Mines.
By R. M. BALLANTYNE, author of "Fighting the Flames," "Silver Lake," etc. With Illustrations. *Globe Edition.* 12mo. Fine cloth. $1.50

"'Deep Down' can be recommended as a story of exciting interest, which boys will eagerly read, and which will give some valuable ideas on a subject about which very little is generally known. The book is embellished with a number of very excellent designs."—*Phila. Ev. Telegraph.*

"The author, through the attractive medium of a well-told story, has managed to give a vast amount of valuable information within a limited space."—*N. Y. Ev. Mail.*

ELSIE MAGOON ; or, The Old Still-House. A
Temperance Tale. Founded upon the actual experience of every-day life. By MRS. FRANCES D. GAGE. 12mo. Cloth. $1.50.

ERLING THE BOLD. A Tale of the Norse
Sea-Kings. By R. M. BALLANTYNE, author of "Fighting the Flames," "Deep Down," etc. *Globe Edition.* With Illustrations. 12mo. Extra cloth. $1.50.

FEW FRIENDS (A), And How They Amused
Themselves. A Tale in Nine Chapters, containing Descriptions of Twenty Pastimes and Games, and a Fancy-Dress Party. By MARY E. DODGE, author of "Hans Brinker," etc. 12mo. Extra cloth. $1.25.

"In the name of many readers, seniors as well as juniors, we thank Mrs. Dodge for a very pleasant and fascinating volume, which cannot fail to be in great demand during the holidays."—*Phila. Press.*

"It is not only useful but entertaining, and just the thing for holiday parties."—*Boston Advertiser.*

www.ingramcontent.com/pod-product-compliance
Lightning Source LLC
Chambersburg PA
CBHW022137020726
47496CB00008B/2443